DELERE PRESS

This paperback edition first published in 2019
by Delere Press LLP

Text © Jeremy Fernando
Images © Adeline Chang
Poem © Lim Lee Ching
Translation © Yvette Yanwen Lim
Layout © Vincent Lee & Sara Chong

First published in 2019 by Delere Press LLP
370G Alexandra Road
#09-09 Singapore 159960
www.delerepress.com
Reg No. T11LL1061K

ISBN: 978-981-14-3678-9

Cotton Candy

text by Jeremy Fernando
alongside illustrations by Adeline Chang
and a layout by Vincent Lee & Sara Chong

with a poem by Lim Lee Ching
translated by Yvette Yanwen Lim

for Abigail, Anaïs, Clover, Dylan, Glenn, Ingrid, Maya, Megan, Meryl, Nael, Sappho, Tykhe, Theo, and Tyler ...

... with all my love ...

with much appreciation to the inimitable Michaela Mullin for her expert, poetic, eye, her musical ear, for so generously reading the tale, for helping me to shape it, to give it shape;

and with thanks to JK Fowler for first believing in its potential;

and with much gratitude to Adeline Chang, Sara Chong, Yvette Yanwen Lim, Vincent Lee, and Lim Lee Ching, for joining me in the madness, for so very kindly indulging me.

She came into being during a conversation — over much whiskey — with Kenny Png and Daniel Sassoon at Quaich Bar: I remain indebted to the both of them for this gift, for bringing her into my life.

/

None of this would have been possible without your good selves.

谁·逐渐被

by Lim Lee Ching
translated by Yvette Yanwen Lim

符号是奇怪的东西。
他说
沉重的真实。
单子风中摇曳
形成三只快乐的手
装饰着笨重的伐木
随着风 吹向
被压制的拼图的尾巴上
其实从来只需要一面旗。

一眨一眨
车头灯亮起
沼泽那一边
沿着海的一带
　（就在他们找到
拴在鼓鼓的漂浮物上
那满塞的公事包

暴晒。盐度过剩。
验尸官如是宣判。）
白天人质交换
并无前例但并非不可行
为了爱着的现实生活中的复活节
兔子。

依然，单子摇曳风中
和信天翁折腾着
还有圣诞节的火鸡
死里逃生闪烁在霓虹灯里

来回的牙线
另一个符号说
当旋转椅开始转动
磨擦，鬼叫着
那复杂的蓝调五线谱音符
飘然而至
伴随着那位说谎偷吃
喝着威士忌的房东的笔迹
沙沙哑哑。

远处，号声响起
没人发现白天亮着的车头灯
因此激怒了巨大的棕榈树和打手们
他们刚奏完十二小节蓝调曲目
穿着破损的鞋，
鞋跟咯咯响。

这故事说得有趣
还未发生已成传奇
谁又会晓得
到处传着的消息不过
什么也不是不过是
真相 – 还有剩下的金箔
旺卡工厂捎来消息：
威利先生无论赏金抑或是巧克力
皆今非昔比。

Cotton Candy

by
Jeremy Fernando

illustrated by Adeline Chang

There's nothing to writing.
All you do is sit at a typewriter and bleed.

— Ernest Hemingway

Said the old man.

It would be too easy if he were out at sea. That, though, belonged to me.
Not that I could sail, nor had anywhere to go.
Drifting away would be too clichéd. So I'll settle for the notion of floating.
Not in any silly existential, or any remotely philosophical, way.
Just floating.

As I sat on the curb, right outside city hall, I kept wondering if cars passing me were always sure of where they were going. Perhaps the drivers had a notion, but aren't drivers merely the operators; managers of a mechanical device, anticipating the collision of steel bodies. That might well, though, be the allure of driving: not just the potential of the accident, but when the car itself takes over.

When the driver is driven.

Sinking
feeling.

Where was he?
was the question that kept repeating itself.

The trouble was, I neither knew his name nor his face: all we had was that
he went by X. Who even remembered the first time they heard his name?
Less was even known of the way the name came to him? Him?

No one could picture his face anymore;
for that matter, where were all the pictures ...

When I passed you in the hallway, you took me with a glance.
You seemed to know who I was looking for. I must have seen you before,
somewhere.

Trouble is I could not picture it —
even as I was looking at you, I was just seeing you.

There is no ~~Always take the~~ *middle*
ground
for us to walk or to take

A sign on the door.

I'll never be sure if I would have seen it if you didn't point it out to me.
You did glance at it. I'm not sure if I saw it, but I can see it now;
I can picture the scene — I can picture seeing it.

The next door called out to me.

Inspector

said the plate.

Could have been a name, or a job description. Maybe even a request. Either way, it looked like a good place to start.

He seemed not to see me.
He pointed to his desk — everything there was marked with an **X**.
I wanted to ask, *where do I find him?* but he never looked at me. I'm not even sure if he ever saw me.

Come to think of it, I had no idea where you were looking.

All I knew was:
I had to find this girl.

It might well have been you.

All day long I think of things
but nothing seems to satisfy.

What was I expecting though:
I had nothing to go on but the fact that I was looking for a girl.
Apparently she likes sweet shiny things. I could stake out all the gift shops
— but in this town, candy was what everybody, anybody, was buying.

That didn't seem to stop my heart from leaping every time I saw a girl with
a box. The glistening, its glow, used to bring joy — now all that gold is
turning to rust.

Happiness ~~in a box~~ *is a warm gun*

Who was writing into, inscribing over, these signs?
Even as they were bringing a little smile to me, I couldn't see a smile.

So I go down to the shop, all shops, any shop. Stumbling around in the dark. Mumbling « girl, sweet girl, girl with sweets … »

I won't sleep 'till I devour you.

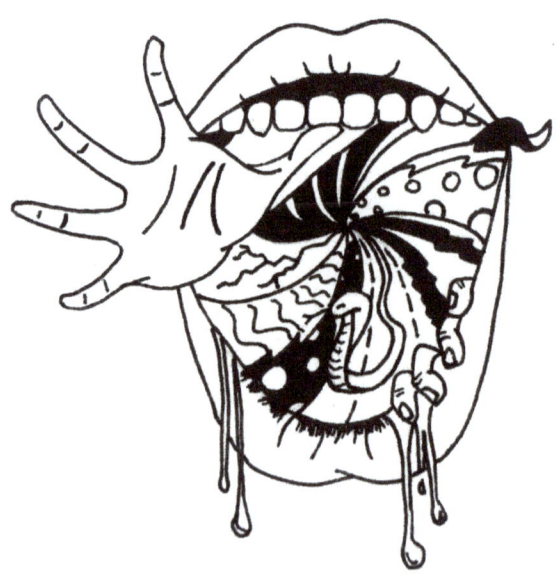

Strange. I can't picture anything but candy. And everywhere I go, all I see is the sign.

I'll melt with you

And people buying.
Candy.

Come to think of it, that was the only thing in colour. As were the people selling them — where did they even come from? All these boys, pretty boys, with angelic tendencies; well, some boys like to act like queens.

Almost like they were being painted there, around me.
They all looked the same.
Silk-screened.

I'll smelt ~~with~~ you ...

Clearly I wasn't the only one who didn't like these signs. Someone else was willing to bleed over them. Them I knew I had to find.

Perhaps, all I had to do was stand around 'till they showed up.
Around one that hadn't been remixed, that is. So I waited.
For a man in a bowler hat no less.

A shimmer of light, a glimmer; then it was gone. It was time to fly.
Breathe.
I guess one shouldn't be afraid to care.
But to where?

Another glimmer.
Nothing to do but follow the light.

So I jumped on.

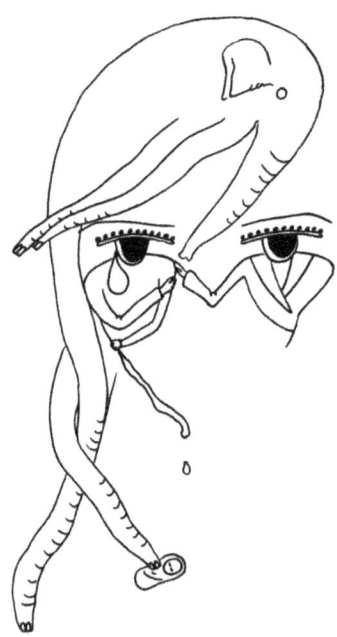

Hanging on in quiet desperation.

A card flies through the light. Into my outstretched hands.

Inebriates we are
Junkies we be
A goblet we carry
in each hand you see

And voices flew in the wind — « follow us, follow us, and you'll soon see
..... what terrors await you in the sea ... »

Hear them I could; but see them, not.
Either they be invisible, or were voices in me head.

« ... watch out the world's behind you;
there's always someone who'll find you ... ».

The rest the wind took away from me.

Where they brought me next
I could not tell.

Not just because I had never been. It didn't even seem to be there. As I was
flying through, places were appearing before me — sketched into the air,
sketched in air just before I landed in them, whizzed through them.

Bouncy, stretchy, light, fast, long;
swinging me through the very phases of their light, their being; seeing
nothing but the fibres between them as I was enveloped within their
clutches, suturing me into them, tasting them as I was caressed by the sweet
delights that floated past me, that I floated in.

The words escape me as I try to speak.
I'm not sure to where they go. Perhaps they have journeys of their own.

But we — nonetheless — arrive.

How, where, what, why — those sort of questions were probably floating in
my head, but they went cloudy after a while.
Much like the air around me.

Thoughts of cotton candy abound again;
I was bound by thoughts again.

A draft of light seemed to whisper to me
and I smiled.

There he was.
A broken king — sitting on a throne that were no longer his.
Atrophied would be the word.

Disappointment was so strong I could taste it.

For, how could this be the man, if one could still call him that; the one that took away everything from me, from them, from us?

But, in taking away our pictures, it seems like they were also taken from him.

He just sat there, looking ... grey.

He clicked his fingers — a shadow danced.
I had never seen her before but I knew she were the girl for whom we were
looking.

When she came in, the air went out,
and the room was filled with doubt.

As she passed through the doorway, she took me with a glance.

I'll stop the world and melt with you.

The pirates, they cried: « come, run, take the last bus home ... »

... but I asked her for a dance ...

As the room spun round and around, the man sitting there started to look different. He was still doing nothing, but it was a nothingness around which everything seemed to spin. And then, there was more; nothingness.

Doing precisely by not doing.

Taste the whip, now bleed for me.

That voice — something was hammering my bones.
Hard to tell if it came from her.
Or him.

But he, he's just sitting there.
Whilst my world is going grey.

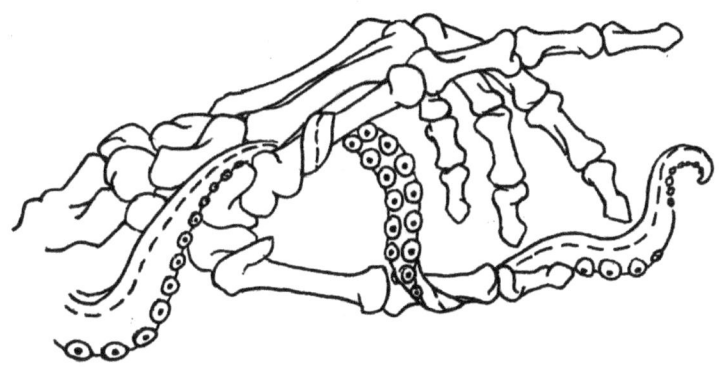

Cotton candy again.
Dancing in my brain. With that strange humming sound. Like I were flying through the air. Only this time I wasn't moving.
And I could even see the card.

That same card ... with that sign.

Melt. Smelt.

Then grey.

الفصل
ٮ

Bleeding. Writing.

My bleeding. His writing.

Who of them will come to be

by Lim Lee Ching

Signs are a funny thing
The one said
Ponderously Real
Sheets in the wind
Made three jolly hands
Deck the lumbering pieces
On a wind up the tail
Of the squelching puzzles
All that was ever needed was a flag

Blink blink
Came the headlights
On the swampy side
Of the coast
(Where they found the
Stuffed brief case
Chained to the bloating floater

The coroner declared sun exposure
And over-salinity)
Daytime hostage exchange
Is a first but can be done
For the love of a real-life Easter Bunny

And still, those sheets flutter
In a battle with the albatross
And Christmas turkey
Close shaves flashed the neon

Floss
Said the other sign
As the rotating chair got into action
Milling and screeching
As the complex blues scale
Enter the picture
Amid scribbles of lyin' cheatin'
Whisky drinkin' landlord
All husky.

In the distance a horn went off
No one spotted the daylight headlights
Thus riling the handlers and massive palms
Who were just exiting their twelfth bar
With worn out shoes
Heels clicking.

Funny how the story is told
Into legend before the occurrence
And who's to know
The message all over the place but
Contains nothing but
Truth – and some leftover foils
From the Wonka plant:
Willy don't make bounty your way
No mo.

Contributors

Adeline Chang is a lover of thunderstorms, idealistic dreams studded with reality, perseverance, and the feeling of rock on bare skin.

Jeremy Fernando reads, and writes; and is the Jean Baudrillard Fellow at The European Graduate School. He works in the intersections of literature, philosophy, and the media; and his, more than twenty, books include *Reading Blindly, Living with Art, Writing Death, in fidelity,* and *resisting art.*

His writing has also been featured in magazines and journals such as *Arte al Límite, Berfrois, CTheory, Full Bleed, Qui Parle, TimeOut,* and *VICE,* amongst others; and has been translated into French, German, Italian, Japanese, Spanish, and Serbian.

Exploring other media has led him to film, music, and the visual arts; and his work has been exhibited in Seoul, Vienna, Hong Kong, and Singapore. He has been invited to perform a reading at the *Akademie der Künste* in Berlin in September 2016; and in November 2018, to deliver a series of performance-talks at the 4th edition of the *Bienal de la Imagen en Movimiento* in Buenos Aires. He is the general editor of the thematic magazine *One Imperative*; and is a Lecturer & Fellow of Tembusu College at The National University of Singapore.

Lim Lee Ching teaches at the Singapore University of Social Sciences. He is the author of *The Works of Tomas Tranströmer: the Universality of Poetry, Pure and Faultless Elation Emerging from Hiding*, and the editor of *The Singapore Review of Books*.

Sara Chong is a realist–figurative painter from and based in Singapore. Her work has been exhibited in group shows in Florence, London, and Singapore, and owned by several private collectors. She is also a commissioned portrait painter. Sara was trained predominantly at the Florence Academy of Art in Florence, Italy, from which she graduated in 2015, with the award for the Best Painting of the Year, and Best Figure Painting of the Advanced Painting Programme. Before immersing herself in classical training, she had a background in illustration, and puppet animation after the Czech masters.

Empathy for the Monster/Beast is the main narrative feature of Sara's work, be it in painting, animation or illustration. Her inspirations are coloured by the affectionate monsters of Odilon Redon, set in the acidic, ominous blue, of the skies of Giorgio de Chirico, and expressed in the hands of Rodin. She paints characters and situations that reflect on the idea of the awkward Beast in the land of beauty. She is ever curious about the concept of the Monster/Beast in myth and daily life, especially where the Beast, most often a cultural or social construct, has its own story and its own rejected version of humanity.

Yvette Yanwen Lim is a strategic communications advisor by day. When she is not designing storytelling strategies for corporates, she spends her free time around good books, learning languages, meditation, music, yoga, and enjoying what little sunshine she gets in Copenhagen, where she is based today.

Vincent Lee is a designer and lover of the arts, fashion, pop culture, and the written word. His interests lie in art direction, marketing, communications, writing, styling, and graphic design. He previously wrote for TODAY Newspaper.